Blacksh[

Revenge Master

Kurt Barker

Copyright © 2017 Kurt Barker

All rights reserved.

ISBN: 9781549576492

DEDICATION

Dedicated to the boys. May you keep getting older but never get old.

CONTENTS

Gunslinger. Mercenary. Killer. Lover.

They called him all this and much more, but like no other in the wild lawless West, the name Tom Blackshot struck fear in the black hearts of outlaws and renegades, and sparked desire in the bosoms of beautiful women. If you were lucky enough to hire the legendary mystery man, no danger was too great and no enemy so deadly that Blackshot could not overcome them. With a gun in his hand or a woman in his arms, Blackshot was without equal.

This is a tale of but one of his many harrowing adventures.

CHAPTER ONE

The faded curtains fluttered limply as a feeble breeze fought vainly against the oppressive midday head. Tom Blackshot stared through them at the clapboard buildings that lined the dusty street a story below. The street was empty and quiet at this time of day, but Blackshot felt an uneasiness gnawing at him for a reason he couldn't place.

"Am I boring you, sugar?"

Candy's voice snapped him out of his reverie. He looked down at her where she knelt in front of him, clad only in thigh-high black stockings. Her strawberry blond hair was piled haphazardly atop her head and her ruby lips curled into a mischievous smile, not two inches away from where her hand held his thick, hard cock.

"You do what you do, and I'll let you know," Blackshot grinned.

Blackshot had helped Candy out of a bad situation with her violent former employer when she first came out West almost a year ago, and today he had happened to run into her again as he passed through town. Candy now ran her own independent service, and Blackshot had a pocket full of money from a job getting rid of some dangerous rustlers for a local rancher, so the reunion had turned into a business deal of mutual benefit.

Candy brought her lips to Blackshot's balls, taking them into her mouth and letting her tongue play across their rough surface. He groaned as she released them from her lips and ran her tongue slowly along his long, rigid shaft until she reached the tip. She teased the head with her tongue, giving Blackshot an impish smirk, then guided it into her mouth and slowly took in his length. Her plump creamy breasts jiggled as she sucked hungrily. Candy had the best body of any of the whores in town, or any of the other towns around it for that matter, so she was always in high demand, but she had been happy to make time for Blackshot. Hell, with a rod like his and the way he could use it, she would have had sex with him for free, not that she was about to tell him that.

Blackshot fingers clenched as Candy's lips worked expertly, and he felt the familiar fire kindling in his belly. He grabbed a handful of her unkempt mane and drove his full length into her mouth with a grunt. She urged his broad head to the back of her warm, wet throat, still sucking vigorously, her hands rubbing his balls. His brain swam as he felt her tongue working in time with his thrusts, bringing him to the verge of exploding. With a groan his hips bucked and his release filled her mouth in a sudden rush. He pulled her head back and drew his pulsing member from her lips, leaving a trail of hot cum spilling down her chin.

"Worth the money?" Candy inquired, licking her lips with a roguish gleam in her eye.

"I'm not finished spending it yet," Blackshot growled. He raised her to her feet and gripping her slender waist, lifted her onto the bed. Candy arched her back and moaned as his broad, powerful hands kneaded her full breasts until they swelled hard beneath his fingers. She spread her soft thighs as he bowed over her, and took hold of his manhood in her hand, slowly coaxing it back to steely rigidity. She guided it toward her until the tip brushed through the strip of dark blonde hair above the warm, wet lips of her entrance.

It was just then that a flash of movement outside the window caught Blackshot's eye, and the sound of hooves clattered in the street below. He glanced out through the curtains and saw a pair of horses drawing up outside the bank at corner of the main street. Astride them were two tough-looking riders; one long and lean like a rattlesnake, and the other a thick bull of a man. As they swung down from their mounts the silver barrels of their revolvers glinted in the sun.

Blackshot looked down at his own black Colts in their oiled leather holsters draped across the chair in the corner. This wasn't his problem. He wasn't he law here. No one was paying him. Besides, he was busy. He looked down at Candy, her soft creamy skin flushed with desire, his shaft poised against her inviting pussy. Almost against his will, his eyes drew away from her and fixed on the window again. He heard the faint sound of breaking glass.

"Just my luck," he muttered, reaching for his jeans.

"Hey! What's the big idea?" Candy cried as he made for the door, still stamping into his boots.

"Don't move from that spot," Blackshot shouted as he slammed the door behind him.

2

Outside the bank, the horses stamped and snorted in anticipation as the doors of the bank were flung open and the two gunmen ran out, one of them stopping to toss a parting word of warning to the banker huddled within.

The other man, the tall wiry one, swung into his saddle. "C'mon, don't worry about that worm," he called, his thin lips twisting into a sneer. "He's scared shitless, like everybody in this hick town."

As his partner mounted up, he touched the spurs to his horse's flanks, and they turned onto the main street at a gallop. That was where they first saw the tall, broad-shouldered man in the flat-crowned black hat. He stood in the center of the street, legs slightly apart, his big hands resting casually on the butts of a pair of black Colts. He raised his head slightly as they pulled up in front of him and met their gaze with cold gray eyes.

"Take it back," Blackshot said quietly. The dust cloud that the horses had raised fell slowly in wisps about his long legs.

"Mind your own damn business!" the wiry man snapped. "You ain't the law around here."

"That is true," Blackshot replied with a humorless grin. "So if you don't put that money back where you found it I won't be bothering with arresting you."

"He's some kinda gunfighter," the burly man said, shooting a quick glance at his partner.

"He was some kinda gunfighter," the wiry man retorted, and his hand flashed to the gun at his side.

He was as fast on the draw as most folks in the West had ever seen, and he had put more than a few men in the ground that had tried to outdraw him, but Blackshot's first bullet was slamming into his chest before he could even bring the revolver level. A second bullet ripped through the bandana around his neck, almost taking his head off and sending him toppling backwards off his mount with blood spraying from his jugular. The horse leaped into a sprint and had passed Blackshot before the outlaw's limp body had hit the dirt.

The second man had hit leather the moment he had seen his partner's hand move, but he was too slow. His gun fired harmlessly into the air as two bullets tore through his guts, spattering the flanks of his horse with blood. He slid sideways out of the saddle and fell to the street, sending the dust into a cloud around him as his horse fled.

"Pretty slick shootin', stranger!"

Blackshot turned to see a heavy set graybeard in a blue suit slowly make his way toward him from the swinging doors of the saloon. A silver sheriff's badge glittered on the man's breast pocket.

"Thanks," Blackshot replied. "Looks like I did your work for you."

"And I'm much obliged to you," the sheriff said. "That's not the sort of trouble I get myself into when I can see it coming."

"Funny attitude for a sheriff."

"That it may be. With the way you handle a Colt I don't reckon you shy away from trouble much. It's a good thing you're on the side of the law, a mighty good thing; and as I say, I'm obliged to you." The sheriff paused a moment and looked down at the dark pools of blood stretching toward each other between the two bodies lying motionless in the settling dust. Finally he said, "So don't misunderstand me when I tell you that you better get the hell out of town if you know what's good for you."

CHAPTER TWO

Blackshot's eyes narrowed. "Come out with it," he snarled.

"You ever heard of Rattler Ragan?" the sheriff inquired.

"I maybe heard the name once or twice."

The sheriff nodded his head toward the body of the tall wiry man. "That would be the former Mr. Ragan," he said. "Mean as a rabid dog, fast as lightning with a six gun, and as ruthless and dangerous as they come. He kept quite a few sheriffs awake at night, and put just as many to sleep permanent like. The other fella's his cousin, Jack. Not as dangerous as Rattler, but plenty close enough."

"Not too much danger to either of them now," Blackshot replied. "What about it?"

"If you're asking that, then I don't suppose you ever heard the name Diamond Dan Ragan?"

"I don't suppose I have. Some relation, I take it?"

"Yes sir, some relation. Diamond Dan is Rattler's pa, and as bad as Rattler was, he was like a choir boy next to Diamond Dan. Hell, the devil himself probably ain't much meaner than Diamond Dan. He and his gang were the terror of every border town from Texas to California back in his day, and now that he's older he ain't gotten any nicer, just smarter. Nowadays he's a regular land baron; or robber baron's more like it. He's got land, money, and a gang that no lawman dares to take on, and once he hears that you put his son in the ground he's gonna use every resource he has to put you in the ground, too."

"Gotta admire a man who loves his family," Blackshot retorted.

"This ain't a jokin' matter, son," the sheriff protested. "There are graves all over this territory with men in 'em that took on Diamond Dan Ragan. You better run, boy, and run fast. Get outta town; hell, get outta the country!"

"I appreciate the advice, sheriff," Blackshot said, "but I'm not much of a runner."

"Suit yourself," the sheriff replied with a shrug. He turned and headed for the doors of the saloon. "Nice knowing you, son!" he called over his shoulder.

When Blackshot returned to Candy's room she was lying on her side on the bed with a worried look on her face. She shook her head as he came through the door.

"My my, you do attract trouble, Tom," she said. "Some day you ought to learn not to meddle in other folks' business."

"Are you joining the sheriff in the advice business?" Blackshot replied. "I like your other business endeavors better."

He unbuckled his belt and tossed his guns on the chair, pulling open his jeans with the other hand.

Candy sat up straight. "Aren't you gonna get outta town?"

"When I'm ready."

"You're a fool to risk your neck for some pussy," she said with a smirk.

"You gonna give me the rest of my money back?"

Candy lay back on the bed and spread her legs. "It's your neck," she laughed.

The laugh turned to a moan as Blackshot filled her with his girth, stretching her to her limit. She grabbed two handfuls of the bed sheet as his strong hands gripped her hips, and wrapped her stockinged legs around his muscular waist. She knew what was coming.

As his thrusts came deep and hard into her hot wet core, her luscious creamy breasts bouncing and wiggling with each impact, Candy looked up into Blackshot's fiery eyes. "It's too bad he's bound for boot hill," she thought to herself. "I'm going to miss this."

The sun had fallen below the rim of the false fronts on the buildings lining the main street when Blackshot made his way down the rickety back stairs and across the dusty lot to the stables. The lantern that hung above the door was burning weakly and he used its meager light to find the stall where his roan was waiting for him.

Blackshot hadn't put much thought to what he would do next now that the job was finished. He hadn't planned much further than Candy, he mused with a smile. Harrison City wasn't far; maybe he'd ride up there and see what jobs were on offer for a hired gun.

He wasn't too worried about Diamond Dan Ragan. He had heard

stories about men like that plenty of times, and usually they were just tall tales. Besides, he'd be long gone from this town before the news ever reached the old bastard.

As he lifted his saddle onto the roan's back, Blackshot caught a shadow dart across the wall from the corner of his eye. Instinct made him jump aside, and the next instant a slug smashed into the wall where he had stood, as the report of a pistol echoed through the stable.

"I guess bad news travels fast," Blackshot muttered.

CHAPTER THREE

Blackshot dove behind a post and rolled behind the wall of the next stall as bullets sent showers of splinters screaming all around him. There were three of them as best as he could tell from picking out their muffled voices through the neighing and stamping of the excited horses, and they had him penned in pretty good. Scanning what he could see of the dusky stables, his eye settled on an alcove by the far wall. A workbench and a saddle rack had been erected within and at the back was a ladder leading up to the hay loft.

Shadows flitted across the wall and the intermittent scuffing of boots on the sawdust floor left no doubt that the men were closing in. Blackshot palmed one of the black Colts, and with his other hand reached for a wooden bucket that lay beside him on the floor, moving it as silently as possible. With a quick snap of the wrist, he heaved it against the post of a stall opposite him. The loud clatter was followed by a shout and a cacophony of gunfire that withered the empty stall. Blackshot leaned out and snapped off three quick shots in the direction of shout, then launched himself toward the alcove, staying low to the ground. Behind him the post where he had been a moment before was crushed in a hail of bullets. As the reports died away he could hear muttered swearing from the far end of the stable, telling him that his shots had done more than just provide cover for him.

As Blackshot reached the alcove he heard heavy footfalls just to his right, and turned to see a big, hard faced man with a black mustache and a short-barreled shotgun bearing down on him, not three feet away. The big man had been trying to cut off an avenue of escape for Blackshot, and had not expected to find himself suddenly face to face with his quarry, and he hesitated an instant before swinging his gun toward the powerful form in front of him. That instant was all Blackshot needed; his hard darted out to the sawed-off barrel and jerked it past him, pulling the killer toward him as the shotgun exploded into action. Blackshot felt the heat of the barrel in his hand as a shower of splinters hit his back. The man's bulk heaved against him, their faces almost touching, as Blackshot pressed his Colt into the man's stomach and emptied every chamber. A fountain of blood and guts spewed out of the big renegade's back as he stumbled backwards and toppled face down into an empty stall, sending up a cloud of sawdust and straw.

Blackshot heard confused shouts behind him as he made for the ladder. It looked old and well worn, and as he gripped it and put a boot on the first rung, an idea sparked in his brain. The corner of the alcove behind the workbench was draped in dark shadows, and Blackshot slipped quietly into its concealment, still keeping the ladder within easy reach. He waited, trying to keep his breathing quiet, until he heard the soft padding of footsteps across the floor nearby. He then reached out a hand to the ladder and pulled it lightly, letting it scrape on the wooden hatch of the hayloft. For good measure he pressed his boot down on the first rung, which creaked heavily under the weight.

Suddenly a voice rang out nearby, "He's goin' up to the hayloft! Cut him off!"

A short, bearded desperado in a buckskin jacket appeared in the entrance of the alcove, aiming a pair of silver revolvers at the empty ladder. The confusion that showed on his face was never satisfied, for an instant later Blackshot's bullet hit him between the eyes, spattering brains and blood across the wall in a wide smear.

Blackshot eased the crumpled body out of the way with his boot and leaned out to scan the room for the last killer. He didn't have to wait long, for from the shadows of a nearby stall a pistol flashed into the light and bloomed with fire, sending Blackshot leaping for cover behind a post. Blackshot fired a shot over his shoulder in the man's direction to make him think twice, then sprang to a post by the back wall of the building and flattened himself against the wall.

As he stood poised and silent, he heard a faint sound behind him. Out of the corner of his eye he caught a hint of movement through the cracks in the boards of the wall. Blackshot dove toward the stall and hit the ground rolling, just as the roar of a shotgun tore a fist-sized hole through the wall where he had been standing. So there were four of them! He twisted onto his stomach and squeezed off a volley of shots into the freshly made hole. From outside he heard a grunt of pain and the sound of something fall heavily to the ground.

Footsteps were approaching fast from the stall where the other man had been. Blackshot could tell by how light the Colts felt in his hands that they were empty. He had to think fast. He jumped to his feet and in a moment he was in the alcove and halfway up the rickety ladder. A bullet snapped the rung of the ladder just below his foot and another splintered the wall behind him, but Blackshot was too fast. He heaved himself up into the loft and rolled quickly against the wall as slugs smashed through the floorboards beside him. He quickly scanned the loft for options, and saw that a pitchfork was resting against the wall just a few feet from him amid the scattered hay. At the far end of the loft a rope hung from a pulley on the ceiling. A risky play, but better than nothing.

Blackshot got to his feet without a sound and took hold of the pitchfork. With his other hand he drew one of his pistols from the holster and tossed it in the opposite direction from the hanging rope. It clattered noisily to the floor of the loft, and an instant later bullets streamed through the floor around it, sending up a cloud of hay and splintered wood.

The man below stood with his back to a thick wooden post, quickly thumbing bullets into the empty chambers of his revolver. A thin trickle of blood ran down his arm from where one of Blackshot's bullets had clipped him earlier. The echoing of the gunshots through the stable had masked the creak of the pulley as the rope had run swiftly through it, so when he caught the sudden glint of light on metal from the corner of his eye, his head jerked up in shock. His mouth opened to let out a shout but it died in his throat as the tines of the pitchfork punched through his gut. Blackshot's powerful arms strained against the shaft of the pitchfork until he felt the tines bite into the wood of the post. The man doubled over with a gasp and tried weakly to raise his gun arm, but Blackshot wrenched the heavy revolver from his fingers. He aimed the freshly loaded pistol at the outlaw's head and unloaded it again.

As the echoes of the gunfire died out Blackshot's ears picked up the clatter of hooves from behind the stable where the fourth man had been. He sprinted to the door of the stable just in time to see the silhouette of a running horse with a bulky rider hunched on its back disappearing around the corner. Blackshot spat on the ground. So he had wounded the last man, but not badly enough. Not enough to stop him from telling Diamond Dan that the hunt was still on.

A small crowd had formed about the stable, not daring to come too close, but peering out from the doorways of the nearby buildings and from behind the curtains of upstairs windows. Blackshot paid them no mind as he reloaded his revolver and returned into the stable to retrieve his other gun and his horse. The roan was pacing nervously at the back of its stall, skittish but unharmed. Blackshot took the reins and led it out into the cool night air.

By now the onlookers had determined that the festivities had concluded for the night, and some had left while others felt safe enough to move closer for a better look at the scene. Through the remnants of the crowd, Blackshot caught sight of the sheriff's hat bobbing toward him. The sheriff approached on unsteady legs, and the odor of alcohol that wafted from him told Blackshot where he had been during the shootout.

"The problem with young men," the sheriff stated in a slurred voice, "is that they do not heed the wisdom of their elders."

Blackshot thought of a few choice words that he could level at the old drunk, but he bit his tongue and swung into the saddle without a word.

"I believe I told you what would happen if you stayed in town," the sheriff continued.

"Well, I'm leaving soon," Blackshot replied.

"That would be wise."

"As soon as I learn where I can find Diamond Dan Ragan," Blackshot said. "I'm going to pay him a visit and thank him personally for setting up that greeting party for me."

The sheriff sighed. "Are you just tired of living, boy?"

"I'm tired of being shot at. It's not something I take kindly to, and I like for folks to learn that."

"Well, you look like the sort of man that knows how to follow a trail," the sheriff said. He pointed with the toe of his boot at that dark spots of blood that dotted the ground along the alleyway where the wounded man had ridden. "I suggest you follow this one if you're determined to meet Dan Ragan, for it is certain that the man who left it is headed nowhere else but straight to Diamond Dan."

"You have been of infinite assistance to me, and for that I am eternally in your debt," Blackshot intoned, touching his hat respectfully. With that he spurred the roan into a gallop and was gone into the night.

The sheriff was not a man to be phased by sarcasm, especially in his current condition, so he ignored Blackshot's parting words and tottered off down the alleyway to seek a little hair of the dog.

CHAPTER FOUR

The morning sun hoisted itself into the purple sky above the rim of the eastern horizon, and Blackshot squinted into it, stifling a yawn. He stamped into his boots and walked stiff-legged through the brush that surrounded his camp, and surveyed the dusty landscape. He had followed the trail left by the wounded man for a few miles before the growing darkness had convinced him to adjourn until the morning.

He had been careful to make his camp far from the trail, choosing a thicket running along a parched arroyo, and even then he had spent the night without a fire. The odds of running into more of Diamond Dan's toughs that night were slim, but no slimmer than that they would have been waiting for him in the stables, and he wasn't going to make the job easy for them by camping in the open.

A little jerky from his saddlebags sufficed for Blackshot's breakfast, and then he was in the saddle again on the trail of the wounded man. The sun was still climbing in the sky and already waves of heat were reflecting off the arid ground. Blackshot guided his horse at a steady pace, keeping an eye out for signs of movement ahead as he followed the trail.

He traveled on across the countryside without incident until the sun had reached its apex and began its slow descent. The trail was easy to follow for an experienced tracker like Blackshot, and he made good time.

As he rounded a bend by a fallen tree, a sudden sound made him pull the roan to a halt. It was a woman's voice. Blackshot looked around warily, sliding a Colt into his palm. He heard it again; a woman crying out in distress. It came from up ahead, beyond a patch of scrubby dry trees at the edge of a gully. Blackshot shook the reins and set the horse moving toward the sound at a slow pace, still carrying the Colt in one hand.

He passed the trees and saw the woman. And what a woman she was! She lay naked on the dusty floor of the gully, her long black hair streaked across her face, her full round breasts heaving atop her slender torso, her firm bronze legs twisted in an awkward position. A torn white blouse and a long black skirt were strewn beside her, and just beyond her Blackshot saw the motionless bulk of a dead horse.

Blackshot swung down from his saddle and made his way cautiously toward the woman. No sound came to his ears save the plaintive sobbing from the woman, and nothing moved in his sight. He knelt down beside her and gently touched her arm. She recoiled at his touch and stared wildly at him with big brown eyes, her plump lips trembling.

"Take it easy," Blackshot said softly. "I won't hurt you. Are you okay?"

"Bandits-- they catch me--" Her voice had a strong Mexican accent. "No one to help me."

"Where are they now?"

"Long gone-- they ride away long ago."

Blackshot tried to help her to her feet but she grimaced in pain and clutched her ankle. "I can't walk," she gasped.

Blackshot looped an arm beneath her legs and the other about her shoulders and lifted her into his arms. She rested her head on his shoulder, her bulging breasts lolling against his hard chest. It was then that he heard a sharp cackle of laughter from behind him. A tall rawboned half-breed Apache with black braids and a scarred face stood on the rim of the gully, leveling a rifle at Blackshot.

"Quite a show, girly! Ya'll ought t'been on stage!" he called with a laugh. "Ain't Consuela done a good job, boys?"

Two other men emerged from the brush on either side of the tall man, one a burly, thick-bearded Mexican, the other a thin weasel-faced man with a dented bowler hat and flecks of gray in his grizzled beard. They both carried pistols aimed straight at Blackshot, and scrambled down to the floor of the gully to surround him.

Blackshot looked down at the woman. Her face was emotionless and she kept her eyes away from his as she pushed out of his arms and hurriedly ran to gather up her clothes. The big Apache regarded her movements with a lopsided grin.

"A fella could get ideas just watchin' the way she moves that ass," he chuckled.

"Ideas that Mr. Ragan wouldn't like too much," said another voice from the brush. A man emerged into the gully; he was stocky and bareheaded, and his unshaven face was pale. Dried blood stained his shirtfront, and one sleeve had been cut away and wrapped tightly like a bandage around his upper arm. A long strip of cloth had been tied over the opposite shoulder to make a sling for his wounded arm. "Keep your mind on the job," he snapped at the tall man.

"Nice to meet you again," Blackshot said coolly. "I didn't get a chance to introduce myself properly last night, but I aim to correct that soon."

"Keep joking, tough guy," the wounded man rasped. "That smart mouth of yours will get shut soon enough."

A heavy revolver barrel thumped into the back of Blackshot's head, and the world disappeared into darkness.

CHAPTER FIVE

When Blackshot came to, the sun was setting behind the far hills. His head ached, and when he tried to move his hands he found them to be lashed tight to a tree behind his back. The tree stood at the edge of a rocky clearing, and behind where Blackshot sat he could hear the faint burbling of a stream, and felt a cool damp breeze off the water on the back of his neck.

A small campfire was crackling at the center of the clearing, and the big half-breed lay reclined beside it on a blanket, picking his teeth with a Bowie knife, the firelight gleaming on his copper muscles. The weasel-faced man sat across from him, gulping down beans from a tin plate with a noisy slurping. Behind them the woman Consuela sat on a log, staring straight ahead with an expressionless face. She was barefoot, clad in the white blouse and long black skirt, and her lush black mane was pulled into a tight ponytail. She did not look at the outlaws or at Blackshot.

Blackshot kicked himself mentally. Women always had been his weakness; especially women with bodies like the one straining against the thin translucent fabric of that blouse. When would he learn? Probably never.

The little man shot a glance at Blackshot and saw that he was awake. He grunted at the Apache and jerked his head in Blackshot's direction. The big man looked over with a smug grin on his thin lips.

"Welcome to our humble abode, Mister Gunfighter," he said in a mocking voice. "I'd offer you a bite t'eat, but seeing as what's in store for you, it'd be a waste of good food."

The grizzled little man let out an amused grunt, sending beans spilling down his chin. Blackshot said nothing.

"Mr. Ragan has a right fun time planned for you," the big man continued. "Now me, I ain't sheddin' no tears for Rattler, but the old man was pretty fond of that dirty devil for some reason, and he means to make you suffer for snuffin' him out."

Suddenly a shout rang out from beyond the brush at the edge of the clearing, "Consuela! Water!"

Consuela jumped to her feet and retrieved a tin pail from the stuff behind the little man and made her way past Blackshot toward the water, her skirt brushing against him as she passed.

The weasel-faced man grinned at his partner. "Duffy don't sound too happy. Chavo ain't exactly gentle when it comes to tendin' wounds."

"Yeah, he ain't lovin' life right now." The big renegade cast a jeering look at Blackshot. "I reckon Duffy is feelin' a little sore that Mr. Ragan wants you brought in alive. He'd like to settle your account himself."

"He tried that," Blackshot growled, "and you see what happened. If that drygulcher wants to give me another crack at putting him in the ground, I'll be happy to accommodate him."

"Consuela! Hurry up, you lazy bitch!!" boomed the pained voice of Duffy.

This brought a hearty laugh from the two men by the campfire. Blackshot heard the soft padding of Consuela's feet as she picked her way up the slick rocky bank of the stream. She passed silently into the clearing, and once again Blackshot felt the soft brush of her skirt against his arm. This time, though, he felt something else as well; something small and hard hit his wrist and landed in the dirt beside him. Blackshot glanced quickly down at his side while the eyes of the men were on Consuela, and saw a small razor gleaming in the fire light! Straining against the ropes, he reached out and swiftly scooped it up before its glint could catch the eye of one of the outlaws by the fire. Moving the small blade into position, he began sawing steadily on the ropes that held him, being careful to show as little movement as possible.

A burst of swearing exploded from beyond the brush, and the half-breed got to his feet with a chuckle. Consuela emerged from the underbrush without a sound and returned to her seat on the log, keeping her eyes away from the men.

"Well, I better fetch them horses. I don't figure to stay here and listen to him holler all night," the Apache said. He drew a finger through Consuela's ponytail as he passed out of the clearing. "Girly gonna have to ride with one of us, seein' as what happened to her horse."

Blackshot recalled the dead horse in the gully and his gray eyes narrowed. Killing a good horse like that was the sort of thing that could ordinarily get Blackshot pretty riled up, but considering that they had the same fate planned for him, he just concentrated all the harder on his work.

The weasel-faced man tossed his empty plate onto the rocky ground by the fire with a clatter. He stood up, wiping his hands on his shirtfront, and walked slowly around the fire toward the log where Consuela sat. He sat down beside her and threw an arm over her shoulder, pulling her close. Consuela didn't look at him.

"Y'know, you and I could get to be good friends now," the man said in a low rasp. "Things are gonna be changing, I betcha."

He slid his hand inside the front of Consuela's blouse and wrapped his fingers around the bare flesh of her breast. He kneaded the the soft mound roughly under the thin fabric, and brought his lips close to her cheek. "The old man ain't keep you away from the boys no more. You're gonna need a good friend like me if you wanna stay all pretty like you are."

Consuela said nothing and continued staring straight ahead. The man's lips twisted into a malicious grin and he jerked the blouse open and pulled the big round melon out into the open. The caramel flesh glistened like bronze in the firelight as it jiggled in the man's hand. "So, why don't you start actin' a little more friendly to me, girly? You want me to keep you away from the boys, don't ya?"

He teased the dark brown nipple between his thumb and forefinger, then squeezed the breast in his hand, letting the flesh bulge out between his fingers. He didn't even have time to let go before Blackshot was on him.

One strong hand clamped over the little outlaw's mouth and the other drove the razor into his bean-stained throat. Blood spurted from his jugular and spattered across Consuela's blouse, dotting her bare skin. Blackshot pressed the blade in with all his might, not relenting until he felt it hit bone. Finally he pulled his hand away from the man's mouth and the limp body slid off the log and tumbled face down onto the dirt. A rush of blood pooled around the man's throat and ran down into the fire in a thick stream, making the flame flicker and pop.

Consuela pulled her wet blouse across her breast but did not look up at Blackshot or at the crumpled form at her feet. Blackshot's hand closed around her ponytail, and her jerked her head back so that her eyes where looking into his. He pressed the bloody razor to her throat.

"Explain," he snarled.

Her dark eyes flared defiantly at him. "I helped you!" she hissed.

"You also set me up to get ambushed in the first place."

"They made me do it. I had no choice. You don't know what they'd do to me if I refused."

"Is that so?" He tightened his grip on her hair and pulled her closer to him. "Sounds to me like Diamond Dan keeps you off limits to these bums, like you've got a special deal with him!"

"You don't understand! It's true, the Patron gives the men strict orders not to touch me," she said, her Latin accent growing thicker with emotion, "but he also gives them very clear orders of exactly what they are to do to me if I disobey or try to run away!"

"What's your story, princess?" Blackshot snapped back. "What's the old son of a whore treat you so special for?"

Consuela's face set in an angry glare. "I was Rattler Ragan's wife," she said.

CHAPTER SIX

"Believe me, no one is happier than I that you ended that devil's life," she continued. "That's why I risk my life to help you."

"We'll discuss this later," Blackshot said. He pulled Consuela off of the log by her hair and dragged her to her feet. He led her stumbling to the tree where he had been bound and pushed her down against it.

"What are you doing?" she hissed.

"Just covering my angles 'til I know the lay of the land, princess," Blackshot replied. He found a segment of the rope that was still a good length, and used it to bind Consuela's hands to the tree trunk. He tended toward believing what she had said, but he wasn't planning to get fooled again. Besides, if Ragan's men got the best of him, it would be safer for Consuela if they thought he had escaped without her help, and tying her up would help convince them that was the case.

Blackshot went to the stuff the men had laid out by the fire, and made a quick search for his Colts. They were nowhere to be found; probably they had left them with his horse when they made camp. He crossed again to where the body of the little man lay; a pistol was holstered at his hip, and Blackshot rolled him over on his side to retrieve it.

"C'mon, let's pack this shit up and get back in the saddle!" The voice of the tall half-breed broke the silence in the clearing, and Blackshot looked up to see the big man stride through the brush. The grin on the Apache's face disappeared as he saw the scene; the blood on the dead man's throat, Blackshot bending over him to reach for his gun, the woman tied to the tree. The firelight flared in his widening eyes as his hand shot to the gun at his hip.

Blackshot lunged over the body of the fallen man with the agility of a panther, and drove his shoulder into the big outlaw's midsection with a heavy tackle. They tumbled together through the dry brush and hit the ground, with Blackshot on top of the other man. The Apache had pulled his revolver clear of the holster, but Blackshot held his wrist in an iron grip. The man's other arm snaked out around Blackshot's neck, but he pulled free while twisting to avoid the outlaw's knee which came thumping into his side. Blackshot brought a hard fist slamming down into the big man's jaw, sending a spray of blood spitting from his mouth. He felt the other man's free hand grasp at his throat, and he pushed it away with a jab of his forearm.

The sound of footsteps crashing through the brush told Blackshot that the struggle had not gone unnoticed by the others. Through the darkness loomed the running figure of the burly Mexican, Chavo. Blackshot caught a glimpse of the grim, bearded face and the flash of moonlight on a steel rifle barrel as he raised it from his side.

Blackshot jerked the Apache's gun hand toward him and closed his other hand over the trigger finger. The pistol spat fire with a roar, and Chavo's body jerked to the side. He staggered forward, then dropped to his knees. He tried to raise the rifle again, but a second bullet hit him right above the eye, sending his hat flying off with part of his head still in it. The Mexican pitched forward, dead before he hit the dirt.

The half-breed's free arm darted upward again, and Blackshot felt his powerful fingers lock around his throat. He tried to twist free, but the powerful grip only intensified. A jerk of the big man's body send Blackshot rolling off of him, and they struggled side by side in the dirt. Blackshot could feel his breath failing as the vice-like grip on his throat tightened. With a lunge he thrust his arm around to the other man's back and drew out the Bowie knife from his waistband. With all the strength he could muster he drove the long blade hilt-deep between the man's ribs. The renegade let out a hollow gasp, and the pressure eased on Blackshot's throat. Blackshot twisted the handle of the knife and didn't pull back until the arm of the other man fell limp at his side and the gun fell from his other hand.

In the darkness outside the clearing, Duffy struggled to his feet from where he lay on a blanket which had been spread for him on the smoother ground down by the trail. He scooped up his revolver with his good hand and stumbled toward the flashes of gunfire. Blackshot had gotten free somehow, he mused bitterly, probably with the help of that sneaky whore Consuela, and was trying to make a run for it. Chavo had run ahead and Duffy assumed that he had put Blackshot down, if the others hadn't already, but hopefully they hadn't finished him off for good yet. If Blackshot was still alive Duffy wanted to put a bullet in the wily bastard to even the accounts between them.

When he reached the clearing, he almost fell over the crumpled body of Chavo. His feet splashed in the pool of blood forming between the bodies of the Mexican and the half breed, who lay motionless with his eyes staring blankly from his scarred face. Blackshot was nowhere to be seen.

Duffy advanced slowly into the clearing, training his gun on every shadow that danced in the firelight. "Come out, you dirty son of a bitch!" he shouted in a wavering voice.

"Your wish is my command, you damn bushwhacker," came Blackshot's rumbling baritone from behind him. Duffy whirled around just in time to see the long blade of the Bowie arc toward him. Blackshot drove the steel shaft into the outlaw's gut with a powerful thrust. The tip of the blade came out his back and poked through the fabric of his shirt. The pistol slipped from Duffy's fingers and hit the rocky ground with a metallic clang. With a strong jerk of his arm, Blackshot drew the blade out again, sending blood spitting from the blade. Duffy slid to the ground like a rag doll and lay still, a dark red stain spreading steadily across his shirtfront.

Blackshot strode over his body and returned to the campfire. Consuela sat where he had left her, a sullen pout on her full red lips, her ample cleavage spilling from the front of her bloodstained blouse. She strained her arms against the ropes and glared at Blackshot.

"What are you going to do to me?" she demanded.

Blackshot merely grinned and crossed over to the tree and split the rope with a swing of the Bowie knife. Consuela pulled the ropes away from her arms and rubbed her wrists, eyeing Blackshot cautiously. Blackshot rummaged amongst the outlaws' gear and found a mostly clean undershirt in a bedroll. He tossed it at Consuela's feet.

"Here. Get that bloody one off you," he said.

Consuela picked it up as she got to her feet, and laid it on a rock beside her. "Turn around so I can change," she said.

Blackshot didn't move. "You've gotten a lot more coy since this afternoon, princess," he said.

Her face reddened and her eyes flared with indignation. "A gentleman would give a lady some privacy to change."

"The next time I meet a gentleman I will be sure to pass on that information to him."

They stood with their eyes locked together, hers blazing with anger, his cold and firm. With a haughty snort, Consuela tore open the front of her blouse. She did not bother to turn away from Blackshot, who watched her big bare tits jiggle and shake as she stripped the bloody shirt from her body. She pulled the thin undershirt quickly over her head and tucked it into the waist of her skirt. Her breasts bulged from every opening, and the thrust of her nipples was evident against the flimsy fabric, but at least it wasn't wet with blood, and Blackshot wasn't exactly going to complain at the sight of it. Consuela stood with her hands on her hips, regarding Blackshot coolly.

"Who the hell are you, and how are you mixed up in this mess?" Blackshot said.

"I am Consuela de Olivera, daughter of Don Joaquin de Olivera. My father was a wealthy man and came from Juarez to settle here and build a ranch. He owned much of the land in these parts until a short time ago.... Until Dan Ragan came."

"And now the land belongs to Ragan, eh?"

Consuela nodded, scowling bitterly. "He did not even bother offering to buy it from my father. He simply murdered him in cold blood, and took everything he owned. There was no one to stop him." She paced angrily as she talked. "As for me, I thought he would murder me along with my father, but he had other plans; Ragan brought some sham of a judge out from the nearest town and made a wedding ceremony and forced me to marry his animal son! That way it was all covered by the law, you see? I inherited my father's estate and now it belonged to my 'husband' and of course, his dear padre! The famous Diamond Dan got to have his cake and eat it too!"

"So you were a prisoner in your own home, and married to the son of the man that killed your father," Blackshot said. "Sounds like you've had a pretty damn rough go."

An imperious light shone in Consuela's eyes. "They couldn't break me. I bided my time and did what I was told. I performed my duties as a wife; yes, even in the bedroom. I put up with it all because I knew one day my chance would come."

"To escape?"

"For revenge."

Blackshot's mouth curved into a wicked grin. "I knew we had something in common."

"I heard the men talking about you," Consuela said, casting a searching look across him, "They talked like you were some kind of demon or something; I could tell they were afraid to come after you. They all bragged that they would defeat you easily, but underneath the bravado they were afraid."

"They were right to be." Blackshot said, jerking a thumb toward the corpses at the edge of the clearing.

"Just who are you, anyway?" she asked.

"The name's Tom Blackshot, ma'am," he said, tipping his hat. "Soon to be known as the man that killed Diamond Dan Ragan."

CHAPTER SEVEN

Blackshot found his trusty Colt revolvers hung across his saddle, which Ragan's men had not bothered to take off his horse's back when they had made camp. He buckled them around his waist and shoved a boot into the stirrup to mount the roan.

Consuela appeared from the underbrush and stood by his horse. Her face was grim and her big brown eyes showed her concern. "There are too many men out there," she said. "They'll kill you."

"They'll try."

"Take me with you."

"Why, so they can kill you, too, princess?"

"Don't call me that again!" she flared, stamping her foot indignantly. "I know the estate like the back of my hand! I can show you how to sneak in without them seeing you. It's your only chance not to die; now take me with you!"

Blackshot flashed a broad smile at her. "I reckon you're going to do what you want to do no matter what I say," he said. "Well, saddle up if you're fixing to. I'm riding and I don't wait for anyone."

Consuela hiked her long skirt up to her hips, and placed her small bare foot atop Blackshot's boot in the stirrup. "I'm riding with you," she said. "I can't the ride these wild outlaw's horses, and the bastards killed my mare. Help me up!"

Blackshot took her outstretched arm and pulled her up onto the stirrup, then put his hands around her narrow waist and lifted her astride the saddle. Instead of climbing up behind him as he expected, Consuela slid herself down in between his legs. Her warm round ass ground against his hips as she positioned herself in the saddle, and it was all Blackshot could do to contain the reaction of his body.

"This is going to be a long night," he muttered, touching the spurs to the horse's flanks.

The last of the sun's rays had been banished from the sky, and a full moon had begun ascending overhead. Its pale light made the path to Ragan's estate easier to follow, and they rode quickly, with Consuela guiding the way. They stayed off the trail, keeping what few trees and bushes there were between them and the open path to minimize the chance of running into another ambush.

Soon a distant light emerged from the dusky gloom ahead, and Blackshot could just make out the silhouette of the broad face of a ranch house.

"We're almost there," Consuela told him in a hoarse whisper.

Blackshot was glad to hear it. He wasn't sure how much longer he could keep riding with that thick, luscious ass bouncing in his lap, before his manhood finally overruled his mind and burst through his jeans.

The light from the estate was showing brighter now, and the long white wall that encircled the ranch house was visible in the moonlight. Through the tall wrought iron gate, Blackshot saw an old stone fountain in the center of a broad courtyard, and a fire was burning in front of it, its reflections sparkling on the bronze patina of a pair of ancient cannons bracketing the gate. Shadowy figures moved in the glow of the firelight, telling Blackshot that several men were stationed in the courtyard.

Consuela pulled on his hand and they slowed to a trot, taking a wide arcing path around the perimeter of the estate until they reached a spot by the side wall where the brush grew thick and close to the stucco wall. Just beyond a tall, sprawling bush that leaned over the top of the wall into the courtyard, they came to a breach in the wall. The plaster had split apart, revealing a deep gash in the bricks beneath which looked just wide enough for a man to slip through. Blackshot eased the horse forward to the shadow of the bush and swung down from the saddle, helping Consuela down after him.

Drawing one of the black Colts from its holster, Blackshot approached the gap in the wall cautiously, and leaned into it to get a view of the courtyard. An old wagon in a state of disrepair stood just to the left of the breach, blocking it from the view of those at the front of the house. The dim reflections from the firelight danced on the pitted spokes of the wheels, and the occasional faint voice could be heard from the direction of the fire. The courtyard by the side of the house facing the broken wall was dark and still, and Blackshot detected no signs of movement.

He slid silently through the narrow breach, and after satisfying himself that there was no one around, he offered his hand to Consuela and helped her through the gap. A lock of hair had escaped her pony tail and fell across her face as she slid through the opening, the curve of her ass rubbing the wall on one side and her breasts bulging from her thin shirt as they pressed against the other wall. What a crime that such a body had been wasted on a bum like Rattler Ragan! The image of the first time he had seen her, naked on the ground, bronze skin glistening in the sun, flashed into Blackshot's mind, and only with an effort did her return his thoughts to the business at hand.

Consuela tiptoed across the sandy ground to the dilapidated wagon and peeked around the corner. Scanning the side of the house, still dark and silent in the moonlight, she whispered to Blackshot, "There is an entrance to the servants quarters back here. Once inside, the back stairs will lead us right to the old devil's room. We can slit his throat and be far away before his gang even knows we were here."

"That sound like a reasonable plan to me," came Blackshot's voice from a distance away. Consuela turned to see him emerging from a wooden shed that stood against the back wall of the courtyard. His eyes flickered with a wicked light, and he carried a dusty keg with the word "Gunpowder" printed across it in faded letters. "Only that ain't the way I work," he said.

Consuela's big brown eyes widened. "What do you think you're doing?" she hissed. "Are you loco?!"

"I saw those old cannons out front when we rode in," Blackshot replied, sitting the keg on the warped boards of the wagon bed. "I reckoned they were mostly for decoration, but I figured a man wouldn't own cannons without also owning the stuff to set 'em off with, just in case he got the notion."

He felt Consuela's little hands tug at his sleeve, trying vainly to draw him away from the keg of powder. "You're out of your mind!" she whispered hoarsely, "You can't fight all those men alone! Every one of them is a killer! We should kill Ragan and get away, far away!"

Blackshot turned and looked into Consuela's eyes. "This was your daddy's house," he said. "It belongs to you now; not to Ragan, not to his gang, not to whichever one of these sons of bitches runs the gang after Ragan's dead. That's the way I see it, and that's the way I aim for it to be."

Tears glistened in Consuela's eyes. "I don't want anything to happen to you," she said softly.

"Get yourself behind the shed and stay there 'til I call for you," Blackshot said with a grin.

Blackshot pried open the keg and let some of the black powder spill out onto the boards of the wagon. He turned the keg onto its side and propped a loose board against its side to keep it from rolling to the front of the wagon. Satisfied with his handiwork, Blackshot slipped to the side of the wagon and put his broad shoulder to the boards. He slowly and steadily applied his prodigious strength to the bulk of the wagon, and the wheels rolled forward with a faint creak. Blackshot drove his legs into the ground with powerful thrusts, propelling the wagon forward at greater speed. As he reached the edge of the house, he jumped aside and flattened himself against the building while the old wagon went speeding along toward the front courtyard.

There were about a dozen men sitting or lounging in the vicinity of the fire, and when the creaking and whining of the wagon wheels came to their ears, they jumped up in alert. Steel flashed in the firelight as pistols were drawn from hips and rifles were brought to bear. The old wagon hurtled into the courtyard and smashed into the stone fountain with a splintering crash. The men approached the wreck cautiously, but not cautiously enough, for they did not see the keg come rolling out of the back of the wagon and into the fire until it was too late.

The explosion shook the house and tore through the camp, sending bodies and parts of bodies tumbling through the cloud of dust and fire that cascaded across the courtyard. The few outlaws that had survived the blast fled, stumbling over chunks of burning stone and severed limbs as they sought to escape the raging inferno. A tall, broad-shouldered form emerged from the thick mist of smoke and dust ahead of them, and white flames burst forth in a roar. The bodies crumpled to the dust and fell into obscurity as clouds of smoke washed over them.

The big double doors at the front of the house burst open, and a half dozen outlaws streamed out into the courtyard with guns drawn. The two men in front were cut down by Blackshot's guns before they realized what was happening. The others scrambled for cover, firing wildly in his direction as they ran. One pitched forward into the fire with blood spurting from his neck as one of Blackshot's bullets beat him to the safety of the stone fountain.

Blackshot circled around the blazing remains of the wagon, running low, keeping the fire between himself and the remaining gunmen as he reloaded the Colts. A tall leafless tree standing not far from the fountain caught his eye, and he made a run for it. As he neared the tree, a burly, tattooed man with a bald head burst from the rolling clouds of smoke, and Blackshot looked down the barrel of a shotgun aimed right at his head. He dove forward as the hot blast tore past his hat brim, and let rip with his own guns as he hit the ground. One slug slammed into the man's hip and the other punched through his kidney, sending him staggering across Blackshot's path and collapsing in the dust by the wall, a trail of blood marking his path.

Blackshot regained his feet and lunged behind the tree just as a bullet smacked into the trunk. Through the billowing smoke he saw the dark form of a man crouching beside the great hulk of the crumbling fountain. Blackshot squeezed off two quick shots at the shadowy figure just as a sharp light flashed from it. A slug slammed into the dirt in front of the tree, sending a shower of dirt across Blackshot's boots, and the dark figure by the fountain tumbled forward and lay motionless as the waves of black smoke covered it.

Blackshot caught a quick flash of movement from the corner of his eye, and turned just in time to see a glistening blade arcing toward his face. He recoiled against the tree trunk, and the knife rushed by him, tearing a long gash in his shirtfront. The muscular, wild-haired man who wielded the blade sprang upon Blackshot before he could bring his guns to face him, and he felt a heavy fist slam into his ear. One of Blackshot's hands was pinned beneath the wild man's knee, but the other one darted up to the wrist of the man's knife hand and held it at bay.

The wild man's free hand came flying toward Blackshot's face again, and only a quick jerk of his head from kept the blow from landing square on his jaw. Blackshot's feet scrambled in the dusty turf until one boot found purchase on a tree root, and mustering all of his strength he drove upward, knocking the outlaw off of him. He jumped to his feet before the other man could recover, and landed a solid kick to the man's midsection, while still retaining his firm grip on the hand that held the knife.

With the man prone on the ground, Blackshot dropped to one knee, pinning the outlaw's arm under him. Then, closing his other hand around the man's fingers that held the knife, Blackshot brought all the power in his thickly-muscled arms down against the other man's own straining strength, and drove the blade into the man's chest up to the handle. When the outlaw's grip weakened, Blackshot took up the slack, twisting the blade home until the man's body went limp, blood gurgling from his chest.

"That's some pretty impressive work," called a voice from behind Blackshot. He whirled around and saw a great hulk of a man facing him, standing with his back to the raging inferno. His face was broad and thick-lipped, and his wavy hair was streaked with gray. With one huge hand he held Consuela in front of him by her hair, and with the other he pressed a heavy pearl-handled revolver to her head. A thin stream of blood trickled from Consuela's lips, but her eyes blazed with defiant anger. "But not impressive enough, you dirty rat bastard," the notorious Diamond Dan Ragan sneered.

Blackshot did not move, stealing a quick glance at the Colts which lay in the dust just a few feet away. The glance did not go unnoticed by the old outlaw. "Don't try it," Ragan barked. "If you think I won't put a bullet through the little whore's head, you're mistaken!"

"I don't care!" Consuela screamed. "Kill him, Blackshot! Shoot through me if you have to!"

A deep rumbling laugh burst from Diamond Dan. "Ain't she a little spitfire? Always good for a laugh. Now get up and move away from them guns-- take care to move nice and slow, boy!"

Blackshot stood up slowly and took a couple of deliberate steps in the direction Ragan indicated. Ragan turned a little, keeping Consuela's body between them, never taking his eyes from Blackshot for a second. Had he looked at the body of the dead outlaw at Blackshot's feet he would have seen that the knife was gone from his chest, but his eyes were trained only on Blackshot.

"I've heard a lot of big talk about the great Diamond Dan Ragan the last couple of days," Blackshot said to the big man. "Mighty tall stories, mighty tall."

Ragan sneered wickedly. "Every one of them true, my boy. You'll see the truth of them soon enough."

"Bullshit," Blackshot scoffed. "If you're such a great man, how'd you turn out a gutless piss ant like Rattler? The little yellow shit begged for mercy before I put a bullet in his cryin' face."

"You lie!!" Diamond Dan roared, his face flushed with fury. "I'll shut your lying mouth right now!" He drew the big revolver from Consuela's temple and swung it toward Blackshot's grinning face.

In an instant the knife flashed across the distance between the two men and struck through Diamond Dan's wrist. He struggled to regain control of his gun, but Blackshot had already snatched up his own pistol from the dirt, and it roared into action. A slug slammed into Ragan's shoulder, making him stumble. Consuela wrenched free from his grasp and leaped aside as another bullet smashed into Ragan's chest. He staggered backward, the flames licking at his boots, his lips moving as if to speak. Whatever he planned to say, he didn't get the chance, for Blackshot's next bullet plowed through Ragan's forehead, sending a shower of blood and brains into the blazing fire. He toppled lifeless into the inferno and disappeared as the flames rushed over his body.

And so the fear of all the borderland, the infamous Diamond Dan Ragan was no more.

CHAPTER EIGHT

Blackshot went to where Consuela knelt and lifted her to her feet. She was sobbing, and she threw her arms around Blackshot and held tight to his shirt as she cried silently against his broad chest. He put his arm around her and led her away from the scene of carnage.

When they reached the porch of the big ranch house, Consuela pushed herself away from Blackshot's body and wiped her eyes.

"I'm okay now," she said quietly. "Are you okay?"

"Everything's okay now," Blackshot replied, gently rubbing his hand across her back.

"Yes, everything is okay now," she repeated slowly. She looked up at Blackshot's face with a new light in her eyes. "Come in. Come inside my house."

She pushed aside the heavy oak doors which still stood a little ajar, and walked into the wide foyer of the house. It was a fine room with plastered walls and a vaulted ceiling, and a wrought iron railing which ran the length of the broad staircase and upstairs balcony. Consuela walked to a table with a carved face which stood near the door, and took a brass bell from atop it. She gave it a shake, sending its ringing echoing through the large room. There was no apparent response, and Consuela rang the bell again.

A wooden door beneath the stairs gave a light creak and a man's face peeked cautiously from its opening. He had a white mustache which stood out against his tanned face, and worry and doubt showed plainly in his eyes. When he saw only Consuela and the tall stranger in the room, he opened the door wider and stepped out into the foyer. Behind him Blackshot saw several other men and women huddled in the shadows of the doorway.

Consuela put down the bell and addressed the man in a confident voice. "Senor Ragan is dead. So are all the vile devils that followed him. I am now mistress of the house again."

Blackshot could tell from the joyous look that spread across the man's face, and the excited whispers from the doorway that the servants of the estate had not been among Dan Ragan's admirers either.

"Oh, Senora Olivera!" the old man cried. "Can this be true? This is wonderful!"

The other servants spilled out into the room with many words of congratulations and gratitude. Consuela held up her hand to quiet them.

"There is much work to be done," she said. "There are many bodies in the courtyard that must be disposed of. The fire by the fountain will serve well for that, I think, but afterwords it must be put out. There are many other matters which must be attended to as well." She turned and motioned to Blackshot. "This is Senor Blackshot, who is responsible for the bodies in the courtyard. He will be staying tonight, so supper must be fixed and the master bedroom must be prepared."

"I will arrange everything," the old man said. "Do not give any of these matters another thought. Leave it all to me."

He led Consuela and Blackshot to the door leading to the dining room, stopping only to lavish many words of thanks upon Blackshot. The other servants gathered around him, bowing and thanking him until Blackshot was quite red faced with embarrassment. He tipped his hat to them several times with a smile as he extricated himself from the throng and went in to supper.

And a fine supper it was! About the only good thing one could say about Dan Ragan was that he liked to eat well, and Blackshot enjoyed the fruits of his pantry all the more for knowing that Ragan would not be enjoying them any further. Consuela's company didn't hurt his mood either, of course.

After supper, Consuela put her arm in his and led him up the stairs to the master bedroom. It was a grand, well-appointed room with a wide carved wood bedstead draped in red silk sheets standing against the wall. Blackshot strolled in, letting his feet sink into the thick carpet.

"So this is my room, then!" he said, taking it all in.

"No, it's not," Consuela replied. He heard the door click shut behind him. He turned and saw Consuela standing naked before him, her clothes in a crumpled pile at her feet. "This is my room."

The flickering candlelight sparkled on her smooth caramel skin; she ran her hands slowly across those big, luscious tits with their hard, brown peaks, then down her ribs that stood out against her taut skin to the hollow of her slender stomach, and finally across her thick, firm hips. Her fingers ran through the patch of black hair between her thighs, and into the wet, glistening lips of her entrance.

"What are you waiting for?" she purred.

Blackshot wasn't waiting. He reached down and grabbed a handful of her bush and pulled her body against him, crushing his lips to hers in a ferocious and hungry kiss. Consuela's mouth responded, kissing him voraciously, desperately. Her lips moved to his chin, then to his chest, as her little hands pulled furiously at his torn shirtfront, practically ripping it open. Her hot, searching lips continued their descent, pressing again and again to the rippling muscles of his abdomen. Her hands were moving, pulling at his belt, then the front of his jeans.

Blackshot felt the pressure growing in his loins and he pushed Consuela's hands away and yanked his jeans down to give himself the relief he needed. Consuela let out a gasp as his long, thick cock burst free and thrust out toward her. She reached out and held the rock hard shaft in her hand, then with a wicked gleam in her eye, she lowered her head and drew her tongue slowly down its whole rigid length.

Blackshot ran his fingers through Consuela's lush black hair, guiding her head downward. She shook her head free and glared up at him, lust burning in her eyes as she lifted her body against his, letting his shaft slide down her chest until it was resting between her breasts. Then she pressed them together with her hands, rubbing the glistening, swollen mounds up and down along the length of his cock, enveloping him in her soft, warm flesh.

A groan escaped Blackshot's lips as he felt his body throbbing against hers. Then Consuela brought her head down again, running her tongue across the head of his cock, then her lips. Blackshot fed his length into Consuela's mouth as her head bobbed back and forth, her lips sucking firmly. She reached around him and gripped his firm buttocks and pulled him to her, driving his shaft down her throat until her chin pressed to his balls. Blackshot felt as if a fire the size of the one in the courtyard was blazing inside him. He buried both hands into her thick black mane and held her head against his body as he thrust his hips into her.

Just when Blackshot knew he could take no more, Consuela pulled back her head and drew his pulsing shaft from her lips. Both her hands closed around the his length and rubbed vigorously. She turned her big brown eyes up to his as she waited, lips parted, until his load exploded in hot waves across her face and into her mouth, streaming down her chin and falling in big white drops across her plump, quivering breasts.

Consuela's hands kept up their work. She raised her cum-streaked face to him with desire still burning in her eyes. "I want you to fuck me," she whispered, his juices running from her mouth as she spoke. "I want you to fuck me harder than I've ever been fucked."

"It's like you read my mind," Blackshot growled. Her took a handful of Consuela's hair and brought her to her feet. He pulled her to the bed and laid her down on the red silk sheets.

Consuela's hands did not release Blackshot's cock for a second. She was panting and her breasts rose and fell on her chest. "At the campfire-- you pulled me by my hair there, too," she whispered hoarsely. "I wondered then if you were going to fuck me."

Blackshot leaned his head close to hers. "I wondered if you wanted me to," he hissed into her ear.

"No, you knew the answer," she gasped, "I wanted you then, and I want you even more now. I want so much to feel you inside me."

Blackshot lifted Consuela's legs across his knee and ran his hands down her soft thighs to the strip of black hair at their apex. He parted her legs and moved between them, letting his cock tease the lips of her pussy. He ran his fingers up her sides to her glistening breasts, crushing the big soft mounds in his hands until he felt them swell hard against his palms. Consuela let out an anguished moan and arched her back, inviting him in.

Blackshot pressed the head of his shaft into her wet warmth, then plunged deeper into her, stretching her with his girth. His hands fastened on her hips and pulled them toward him as he strained against her, until his whole length was filling her hot core. From the expression of shock and ecstasy on Consuela's face, Blackshot could tell that no man had ever been this deep inside her before.

"Now! Take me now!" she cried, her hand pressed to her stomach.

Blackshot thrust hard into her, strong and fast, his powerful arms grinding her thick hips into the impact of each drive. Her bulging tits rolled and bounced on her chest as he hammered into her repeatedly, his balls slapping against her voluptuous ass cheeks with each thrust. Consuela let out a guttural cry as a powerful orgasm rocked her body. Her back arched and her heels dug into the back of Blackshot's straining thighs, and then relaxed.

Blackshot wasn't stopping, however. Still punching his cock steadily into Consuela's mound, he swung her leg across his body, rolling her onto her stomach. He took a handful of her raven hair and wrapped it around his hand with a deft swing of the wrist, giving him a firm grip. He gave a yank, pulling Consuela's head back and arching her back, allowing him to penetrate her deeper. Digging the fingers of his other hand into her sweaty hips, he went to work, pounding her pussy like a jackhammer.

Consuela gave a whimpering moan as another orgasm washed over her; her hands clutching the red silk so tight her fingers were white, her legs writhing. Blackshot could feel that he was reaching his limit as well. He slid his rigid length from her wet sheath and released his grip on her hair. She buried her face in the sheets as he stood over her, letting his shaft rest between her thick, glistening ass cheeks. His hips bucked against her, and he sent hot jets of cum crisscrossing the whole of her back and ass.

Blackshot collapsed onto the bed beside Consuela's wet body, and they lay together without moving for what seemed like an eternity, the heavy panting of their breaths the only sound, as the room spun around them.

The first purple streaks of dawn were mixing with the hues of the night sky when Blackshot arose from the bed, sliding gently to the floor so as not to wake Consuela. He gathered his clothes from where they had been strewn in the haste of the night's action, and tiptoed toward the door.

"Where do you think you're going?" demanded Consuela's sultry voice from behind him.

She jumped up from the bed and ran to the door and blocked it with her naked body, holding the brass handle behind her back.

"You forget, I am the mistress of this house now!" Consuela said with a mischievous smile. "And if you want to leave this room," she turned to the door and placed her hands against it, bending slowly forward and spreading her supple brown legs wide, "you'll have to get through me!"

It was the second time that night that Blackshot had been held captive, but this time he did not mind at all.

ABOUT KURT BARKER

Kurt Barker, formerly of Florida, Georgia, Indiana, Connecticut, North Carolina, West Virginia (and maybe a few others he's forgotten about) now resides in Virginia with his family, and spends his time writing action and adventure stories for fun and (when all goes well) profit.

19163689R00026

Printed in Poland
by Amazon Fulfillment
Poland Sp. z o.o., Wrocław